Vocable Quiz

ANGLAIS

Vocable

QUIZ anglais

Judy Martinez et Sasha Hourwich
illustrations
Cotten
Anne de Courseulles

Le Livre de Poche

Comment se servir de ce quiz

Vocable Quiz anglais est un livre de jeux et d'exercices pour réviser ou découvrir les principales règles de la grammaire anglaise. Il est destiné à tous ceux qui veulent rafraîchir leurs connaissances, réviser leurs bases ou tout simplement se tester.

Conçu dans un esprit ludique, tout en couleurs, il fait la part belle aux illustrations pour donner vie aux différents types d'exercices : QCM, vrai/faux, exercices à trous, mots croisés, jeux phonétiques...

Cet ouvrage est divisé en 12 kits, du plus simple au plus difficile. Chacun raconte les aventures linguistiques d'un routard parti, sac à dos, à la découverte du monde anglophone : balade irlandaise, frénésie new-yorkaise, Far West américain, bush australien... **Vous apprenez ainsi un anglais varié, riche de ses particularismes culturels.**

Chaque kit peut s'étudier indépendamment des autres en fonction de vos besoins :

- **Lisez attentivement les règles de grammaire figurant en première page.** Concises et précises, elles sont illustrées de nombreux exemples pour compléter les explications.

- **Faites les différents exercices de grammaire proposés**, calculez votre score en bas de page et vérifiez ainsi que les règles sont bien comprises.

- **Entraînez-vous aux jeux de vocabulaire.** Jouez avec les mots et mémorisez ainsi le vocabulaire de nombreuses situations de la vie courante.

- **Amusez-vous avec les jeux inédits de phonétique.** Un excellent moyen d'améliorer naturellement votre prononciation.

- **Testez-vous à la fin de chaque kit** pour vérifier la bonne assimilation des règles.

- **Et enfin, reportez-vous aux corrigés en fin de volume** pour contrôler vos réponses.

Et maintenant, faites vos jeux !

Nous vous souhaitons un excellent apprentissage en notre compagnie.

Table of contents

Kit 1

present continuous

- **to comment on an action you can see:**
Look! I'm sunbathing on the beach.

- **to comment on a future action (with a time indicator - tonight, tomorrow, next year...)**
We're coming home tomorrow.

- **to describe someone and their attitude:**
See that guy over there? He's wearing glasses. He's holding a glass of white wine and he's talking to the girl who is sitting down.

- **to show irritation:**
I'm always forgetting New Zealand is not like Australia.

- **to talk about changing situations, trends and events:**
More and more people are emigrating to New Zealand.

present simple

- **to talk objectively about someone's habits and characteristics:**
He goes to New Zealand every two years to see his family. However, he emails them every day.

- **to talk about a generalisation or a constant fact:**
New Zealanders speak English.

- **with certain verbs to talk about feelings and opinions:**
New Zealand seems a great place to live. You don't need lots of money to live there.
New Zealanders don't believe in superficial things.

A AN THE Ø

- **"a" is used:**
- to generalise in front of a countable noun: *She gave* ***a*** *speech about life in Australia.*
- to talk about someone's job or condition: *He's* ***a*** *flying doctor.*
She's ***a*** *business woman.*

- **"an" is used in front of nouns beginning with a vowel or an "h" when it's not pronounced.**
An *hour,* ***an*** *enemy...*

- **"the" is used for particular items:**
Compare:
I like cars. / I like ***the*** *car you bought last week.*
She loves life. / She especially loves ***the*** *life she leads in New Zealand.*

- **Ø is used:**
- to generalise in front of an uncountable noun:
There are lots of animals in Ø New Zealand.
- in front of certain names:
He is Ø Professor Jenkins.
Ø New Zealand nurses often go to the UK to work.

two presents

Freddy sends his mum SMS messages from New Zealand.

Choose between the present simple and the present continuous to complete his messages.

ANNE DE COURSEULLES

1. I am walking/walk through the forest.

2. New Zealanders say/are saying "tramping" not "walking"!

3. People are calling/call New Zealanders Kiwis.

4. New Zealanders like/are liking to be called Kiwis.

5. Sheep are grazing/graze everywhere in New Zealand.

6. I'm talking/I talk to a sheep.

7. Jill enjoys/is enjoying herself.

8. She loves/is loving going on holidays at the seaside.

9. New Zealanders are using/use plastic money.

two presents

10. You are being able/are able to wash New Zealand money.

11. Bill is tasting /tastes some delicious new wine.

12. New Zealand is making/makes great wines.

13. Jill is jumping /jumps off the bridge.

14. New Zealanders constantly are inventing/invent new dangerous sports.

15. We come/are coming home tomorrow.

16. It feels/is feeling like we arrived here yesterday.

17. Jill wants/is wanting me to send you her love.

17
SCORE

Continuous and simple verbs and words

Classify the verbs into two groups: those used in the simple and continuous form (action verbs) and those not normally used in the continuous form.

- believe
- belong
- dance
- dream
- hate
- have fun
- hear
- look at
- look for
- love
- manage
- own
- run
- see
- speak
- think
- understand
- walk

Action verbs (used with both presents)	Verbs to talk about feelings or opinions (present simple)
....	....
....	....
....	....
....	....
....	....
....	....

Which of these words can be used with the present continuous and which with the present simple?

- always
- at the moment
- never
- now
- often
- sometimes
- tomorrow
- tonight

Present continuous words	Present simple words
....	....
....	....
....	....

26
SCORE

a, an, the, Ø

▸ Circle either A, AN, THE or Ø

1. A AN THE Ø Prime Minister of New Zealand is A AN THE Ø woman.

2. A AN THE Ø New Zealanders care A AN THE Ø lot about A AN THE Ø environment.

3. A AN THE Ø large part, 80% of A AN THE Ø population, lives in A AN THE Ø cities.

4. A AN THE Ø people enjoy A AN THE Ø good lifestyle in one of A AN THE Ø world's most attractive regions.

5. A AN THE Ø capital is Wellington, A AN THE Ø city considered to be A AN THE Ø exciting place to visit.

6. A AN THE Ø climate is sub-tropical in A AN THE Ø north and continental in A AN THE Ø mountains in A AN THE Ø south.

7. A AN THE Ø eight largest cities of New Zealand have A AN THE Ø project to maintain A AN THE Ø quality of A AN THE Ø life in A AN THE Ø largest metropolitan centres.

8. Can you imagine living in A AN THE Ø beach house just A AN THE Ø few miles outside A AN THE Ø main city centre?

9. A AN THE Ø estimated 85% of A AN THE Ø New Zealand's plant species are native to A AN THE Ø islands because they had so little A AN THE Ø contact with A AN THE Ø rest of A AN THE Ø Pacific islands.

10. New Zealand was once not A AN THE Ø island but A AN THE Ø fragment of Gondwana, A AN THE Ø super-continent that embraced both Australia, Antarctica, parts of A AN THE Ø South America, and A AN THE Ø Indian subcontinent.

37
SCORE

travelling words

The Browns are off to New Zealand.

Complete the sentences about the drawings with the right words

pack, take off, spend, rush, pick them up, delay, board, land

1. The Browns are .... their suitcases.

2. The Browns are .... to the airport. They are very late.

3. However, when they get to the airport they must wait. There is a two-hour ...... due to fog.

4. The Browns are .... the plane.

5. The plane is .... at last.

6. Eighteen hours later they are .... in New Zealand.

7. The hotel courtesy car is .... They are .... the night in a comfortable bed. They are exhausted.

	8
SCORE	

'i' sound wheel

Use the letters in the box below to find the words in the wheel.

Part of each word has a vowel sound like the "i" in ship.
For an extra point, circle this vowel sound.

Here are the words in the puzzle:

virtape	lidub	aseegms
nussibes	timune	galveil
terpyt	algguena	
antinmuos	wenom	

1. the B in MBA
2. could you wait just a ...., please?
3. what you save first along with children
4. to construct
5. opposite of ugly
6. something you send & receive on a cell
7. not public
8. smaller than a town
9. something to climb
10. what you speak

24
SCORE

Test yourself on kit 1

Right or wrong?

	right	wrong
1. **My sister is living in New Zealand** means my sister is not staying permanently in New Zealand.	❑	❑
2. You use the PRESENT CONTINUOUS to talk about general facts: **Earthquakes are happening a lot in New Zealand.**	❑	❑
3. The PRESENT CONTINUOUS can be used in the future: **We're visiting Rarotonga next year.**	❑	❑
4. **New Zealanders are rearing a lot of sheep:** this is a constant fact which never changes, hence, we use the PRESENT CONTINUOUS.	❑	❑
5. The PRESENT SIMPLE is used to describe somebody: **The person over there wears glasses, stands and reads a newspaper.**	❑	❑
6. **Look, my sister has fun in New Zealand** is correct.	❑	❑
7. You don't use **'the'** in front of names of meals: **What time is dinner?**	❑	❑
8. You use **'the'** in front of names of languages: **She speaks the English really well.**	❑	❑
9. You can only **SPEND** money not time.	❑	❑
10. A **DELAY** often makes you late.	❑	❑
11. The last syllable of **MOUNTAIN** is pronounced TIN.	❑	❑
12. The second vowel in **MINUTE** is pronounced the same way as the first one. We say MINIT.	❑	❑

	12
SCORE	

Quantifiers

Some, any, no

are used in front of countable or uncountable nouns in the plural.

Some is used
- in an affirmative sentence:
There is some milk in my tea.
There are some sugar lumps in my tea too.
- in questions when you expect the answer to be yes: *Do you want some tea? Of course I do.*

Any is used
- in a negative sentence:
I don't want any tea now, thanks.
- in a very general way :
You can find any type of food you want in the restaurant.

No **is negative and is used with a positive verb:** *There are no customers today.*

much, many, a lot of

Much and many are often used **in negative sentences and questions in front of countable or uncountable nouns in the plural.**
There isn't much sugar in the bowl. There aren't many cups on the table.

A lot of is used **in affirmative and negative sentences and questions in front of countable or uncountable nouns in the plural.** So, if you don't know whether to use MUCH or MANY use A LOT OF or LOTS OF.

Compare the use of quantifiers in this table

Uncountables like *MILK*	Countables like *BOTTLES OF MILK*
*There **is no** milk.*	*There **aren't any**/There are **no** bottles of milk.*
*There **is little**...*	*There **are few**...*
*There **is a little**...*	*There **are a few**...*
*There **is some/isn't any**...*	*There **are some/aren't any**... There are several ...*
*There **isn't much**...*	*There **aren't many**...*
*There **is a lot of/lots of**...*	*There **are a lot of/lots of***
*There **is plenty of**...*	*There **are plenty of**...*
***Most of** the milk **is** fresh.*	***Most** bottles of milk/**Most of** the bottles of milk are fresh.*
***All** the milk **is**...*	***All** the bottles of milk **are**...* ***Each/Every** bottle of milk **is**...*

Learn these composed words by heart

Words referring to **people:** ***Somebody/anybody/nobody***
Words referring to **things:** ***Something/anything/nothing***
Words referring to **places:** ***Somewhere/anywhere/nowhere***

quantifiers

Some • any • much • many • a lot of/lots of • plenty • few • most • most of

Complete this history of Hay-On-Wye in Wales by choosing the right word.

1. Hay-on-Wye is a town that lies on the border of Wales and England. Because of its position the town has seen quite a many/much/lot of battles.

2. In the early 60s Richard Booth opened an antique store in Hay-on-Wye where he also sold any/some/much books.

3. He couldn't sell some/any/much antiques but he did sell much/any/a lot of books.

4. There were few/plenty/much of empty shops along the high street of Hay-on-Wye and Richard Booth bought most of them.

5. There have never been as many/lots of/much supermarkets as bookshops in Hay-on-Wye.

6. Most/most of/few the shops in Hay-on-Wye sell books.

7. Most/most of/few tourists go there to buy books.

8. Richard Booth made many/a lot of/plenty money and bought the ruins of a local castle.

9. Most/the most/few of it got destroyed in a fire in 1980 and he had to sell any/much/some of his shops because he didn't have any/much/some money.

10. But Hay-on-Wye is still famous for having the most/most of/few bookshops in one small town.

11. You can find any/plenty/some book you want there.

14
SCORE

quantifiers

Complete Brigitte's conversation with Megan about Wales. Use these words: somebody • anybody • nobody • something • anything • nothing • somewhere • anywhere • nowhere

1. Brigitte - Is there .... in Great Britain that can count more traditions than Wales?

2. Megan - No, ... else in Great Britain has as many traditions as Wales.

3. Brigitte - Is there .... I should see when I go there, an event perhaps?

4. Megan - There is .... that is very famous and especially worth seeing: the Eisteddfod.

5. There is .... like it anywhere else in the world. It is a large scale folk festival.

6. Brigitte - .... told me it was a competition too. Can .... go?

7. Megan - Of course. It is an event .... should miss. Are you going to go?

8. Brigitte - Definitely. Can you give me the address of .... nice to stay?

9
SCORE

Let's go down the pub

Do you know what to say in a pub? We've given you the words but we've forgotten the vowels. Can you put them in?

1. When you order beer, you ask for a H_L F or full P_NT.

2. The man who owns the pub is the L_NDL_RD.

3. If the service is good, you leave a T_P.

4. When it's your turn to buy the drinks, you say, "Okay, it's my R_ _ND."

5. The normal type of beer people drink is called L_G_R.

6. If it doesn't come in a bottle it is DR_ _GHT beer.

7. You can also order SP_RKL_NG or F_ZZY water.

8. If you offer to pay for someone, you say, "Let me TR_ _T you."

9. If you're hungry, you can order the D_SH of the D_Y.

10. You can also ask for a C_RRY.

11. You also need to take the knives and forks to your table. You say, "Can I have some C_TL_RY?"

12. For dessert, you look for the SW_ _T trolley.

13. A typical dessert is a TR_ FL_.

14. At eleven p.m. the pub will start to close. The barmaid will say, "L_ST _RD_RS, please."

16
SCORE

Welsh SOUNd puzzle
The sound eeeee

▶ All the words have the vowel sound of TEA

If you go walking in the country in Wales,

1. You can see white wooly animals known as S.....
2. and their lambs are often sold as M.....T.
3. If you go to a pub, you have a B......
4. Take a S..... on a bench
5. and watch the rugby T..... on the telly.
6. You won't spend much money in Wales because things are C......
7. You can also try to get to the P..... of Mount Snowden
8. if your F..... don't get too tired of walking.
9. You will see how friendly P..... are.
10. Everyone you M.....
11. in the village will G..... you with a nice "Hello.
12. and ask you how you F......
13. At the end of your stay, you won't want to L......

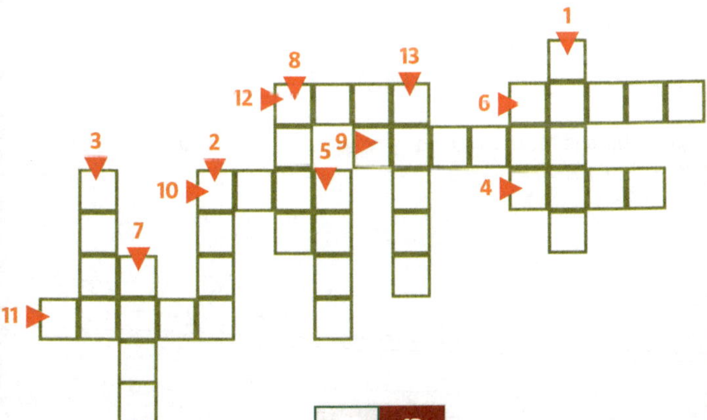

13

SCORE

Test yourself on kit 2

Right or wrong?

	right	wrong
1. You can replace MANY or MUCH with A LOT OF.	❑	❑
2. There isn't many people in the pub.	❑	❑
3. He went to the pub and had a little beers.	❑	❑
4. After plenty to drink they went and had a meal.	❑	❑
5. They bought any books in Hay-on-Wye.	❑	❑
6. They didn't want no antiques.	❑	❑
7. They had never seen nowhere like that town before.	❑	❑
8. They had never seen anything like it.	❑	❑
9. A lager is a typical English dessert.	❑	❑
10. MEET and MEAT do not have the same vowel sound.	❑	❑

SCORE ___ / 10

simple past

formation

• Add 'ed' to a verb to form the simple past:
look → looked
talk → talked

• Some verbs are irregular:
do → did
find → found

• Some have the same form as the present simple and the infinitive:
cut → cut
put → put

We need to learn the irregular verbs by heart.

questions & negatives

• Form questions with DID and the basic verb form:
Did you see her this morning?

• Form negatives with DID + NOT and the basic verb form:
No, I didn't see her.

uses

• to refer to an event and a time in the past: *I talked to him the other day.*

• To be precise about the time in the past:
I saw the movie last night with a friend.

• when using a specific date:
I came back from Germany in 1955.
I lived there three years ago.

relative pronouns

who, which, that, ø

• Who only refers to people whereas that and which can refer to objects and people:
Who said that?

• Which is used when referring to an object. It can be replaced by that or ø:
Where's the record I lent you? =
Where's the record which/that I lent you?

Which is also used when there is a choice between two or more things or people:
Which of those people do you know?

what, whose

• What = the thing that. It announces what follows:
Did you hear what they said?

• Whose is used in a relative clause instead of his/her/their:
That's the person whose car I'm using.

simple past

The poor lonesome cowboy

is in jail in Texas and writing to a friend in North Dakota. Correct his letter.

Yesterday I goed into town and seed my girlfriend

....

She thinked I was coming later in the day, so she

....

been not home. I breaked down the door and finded

....

that there was no one there. So I leaved the

....

house and rided my horse to the saloon. I drinked a whisky and then another one, and by the end of the day I getted very drunk. I was very hungry too, so I buyed myself a big juicy hamburger with onions and ketchup. I eated it very quickly because two guys beginned arguing and they fighted with each other over a girl. I understanded that it was my girl they were talking about, so I throwed myself into the fight too. The sheriff putted me in prison and that's where I am now.

17
SCORE

Jesse James

Complete the story about Jesse James by choosing the right verb and conjugating it correctly in the past.

begin • learn • justify • put • commit • frustrate • rob • kill • meet • stand • give • be • join • attack • make off • rob • be

1. Jesse James .... born on September 5, 1847, in Kearney, MO*.

2. During the Civil War, the teenager James .... a band of pro-Southern guerrillas.

3. He .... the art of being an outlaw.

4. He .... Union supply trains and depots.

5. This notorious band of guerrilla fighters in Missouri .... many atrocities.

6. They .... their actions by saying that they were fighting on the side of the Confederacy.

7. Following the war between the states, the young Jesse James .... together a gang of some of the most notorious, yet celebrated names of the American West.

8. This new gang .... a massive crime spree that .... law enforcement officials in the Midwest.

9. They .... the Clay County Savings Association in Liberty and .... with $62,000.

10. The gang .... banks and .... many who .... in their way for the next eight years.

11. The James Gang .... not a bunch of cold-blooded killers and .... money to those they .... along the trail who were less fortunate than they were.

* Missouri

17 SCORE

American inventions

▸ Put the relative clause in the right sentence.

1. Alexander Graham Bell was the man ....

2. The electric light bulb .... was finally patented in 1895 in America.

3. Thomas Alva Edison .... lived in New Jersey.

4. The most famous sewing machine .... was invented by Isaac Singer in the middle of the 19th century.

5. The first practical telegraph line .... was invented by Samuel Morse.

6. A device .... was first invented in 1893.

7. When Bill Gates founded Microsoft in 1975 very few people knew ....

8. Do you know ....

9. The I-POD .... is considered by some to be Apple's most brilliant invention.

10. Jeff Hawkins invented the palm pilot and did ....

ILLUSTRATIONS: ANNE DE COURSEULLES

a. which you can use to store lots of music

b. that someone nicknamed the 'Zipper'

c. which ran from Baltimore to Washington, DC,

d. who invented the telephone.

e. what we all would like to do: come up with a totally useful machine.

f. what a computer could be used for.

g. whose inventions include the electric light and the gramophone

h. which was first invented in England in 1800

i. which computer was the first user-friendly one: PC or Apple ?

j. that we know and love

	10
SCORE	

short action verbs

Make words from short action verbs› Find words with the same roots.

We've given you a definition and now you put in the empty boxes words which are based on the 'root' word.

drop

a small amount of liquid	someone who leaves school or college before finishing their studies	a little tube used to measure and distribute small amounts of a liquid

pick

a small truck used for fast deliveries	difficult to please	money you can make easily in a business or an activity

shake

a container used to make cocktails	a major change usually in an organization	uncertain, doubtful or not sure to succeed

lay

a person who is not trained or experienced in a subject	the composition or arrangement of a design or a page	a redundancy or a time when people stop working

hold

a container	a type of corporation	a raid or robbery

break

the first meal of the day	delicate	when the sun starts to rise

18
SCORE

Sound Puzzle

Past endings

Put the verbs below into the past and then put them into the three circles, according to how the past endings are pronounced.

- arrive
- ask
- discover
- distribute
- finish
- hate
- imagine
- launch
- lick
- link
- love
- market
- open
- part
- pick
- touch
- visit
- wait
- watch

't'

'd'

'id'

19

SCORE

Test yourself on kit 3

Right or wrong?

	right	wrong
1. You make the simple past tense by adding **'ed'** to the majority of verbs.	❑	❑
2. To **make a negative sentence in the simple past** you put the verb and the auxiliary in the past: **I didn't went there.**	❑	❑
3. Did you find all the papers you said you needed?	❑	❑
4. Questions in the past are made by inverting the verb and the subject and then adding the auxiliary: **Went you there ?**	❑	❑
5. I was been in the States four years ago and I thinked it was great.	❑	❑
6. She cut a beautiful design in the silk in order to make a dress.	❑	❑
7. He was the man which invented the computer.	❑	❑
8. The car what you bought looks fantastic.	❑	❑
9. The past tense of start, stop, want, ask all have the soft 't' pronunciation.	❑	❑
10. A person with no expertise is a **layout** man.	❑	❑

	10
SCORE	

present perfect simple

reflects the point of view of the speaker.

The speaker is not interested in when the event happened but in the present time result.

- **It is used to explain the present.**

He has been to Scotland a lot. That's why he likes whisky.

- **It is used to talk about events that have just happened.**

I've just got a job in the Scottish Highlands.

- **It is used to talk about an event that happened in the past but the date is unimportant.**

I've been to Scotland. (It means the person speaking knows Scotland well.)

present perfect continuous

is a link between the past and present.

- **It is used when you want to emphasize that the event started in the past and is happening now and is not finished.**

They've been living in Scotland for quite a while.

- **Learn these questions by heart:**

How long have you been working in this company?
How long have you been talking on the phone?

present perfect words: since, for, yet, already

These words are often used to express the present perfect 'idea'.

FOR **is used in front of a number of years, hours etc:**
*The Scots have had their own government **for** 6 years.*

SINCE **is used in front of a precise date or time:**
*Devolution has been in place **since** 1999.*

ALREADY **is used to show something happened earlier.**

YET **is used in the negative to show that something didn't happen for the moment but will probably happen in the future:**
*Devolution has **already** taken place in Scotland but it has not happened in Wales **yet**.*

Other words used with the present perfect:
RECENTLY, ALWAYS, NEVER, JUST...

present perfects

Choose the right answer

Driving in the Scottish Highlands Jim and Chris are lost. Choose the right answer according to the first sentence.

1. Do you know where we are?
a ❑ Of course not. I never went here in my life.
b ❑ Of course not. I have never been here in my life.

2. Well, look at the map.
a ❑ I haven't seen a map anywhere in this car.
b ❑ I didn't see a map anywhere in this car.

3. Why didn't you bring one?
a ❑ I've forgotten.
b ❑ I forgot.

4. I thought you used to live near here.
a ❑ I have lived nearby when I was a baby.
b ❑ I lived nearby when I was a baby.

5. Shall I turn left here or drive straight on?
a ❑ Turn right. We've already been past this pub three times.
b ❑ Turn right. We already went past this pub three times.

6. Do you want to drive? I'm exhausted.
a ❑ Why? You haven't been driving long.
b ❑ Why? You didn't drive long.

7. Okay, give me the wheel. Where is reverse gear?
a ❑ Come on! You are kidding me. Haven't you ever been driving this sort of car before?
b ❑ Come on! You are kidding me. Haven't you ever driven this sort of car before?

8. There's a hitchhiker. Excuse me, if we give you a lift can you show us the way to Ben Nevis?
a ❑ Och aie! *('Yes' in Scottish!)* Thank you. I've been here yesterday and waited for someone to pass by. You are the first car I saw.
b ❑ Och aie! *('Yes' in Scottish!)* Thank you. I got here yesterday and have been waiting for someone to pass by. You are the first car I've seen.

8
SCORE

Fill in the gaps

with the right present perfect word below.

- always
- for
- yet
- already
- since
- recently
- never
- just

1. Judy - My sister has . . . . moved into a castle in Scotland.

2. Sasha - Does she like it? I've been living in an old flat in Edinburgh . . . . 1997 and I love it.

3. Judy - Well, she hasn't been there long and she has . . . . seen two ghosts.

4. Sasha - Two ghosts! You are kidding me! I've . . . . seen a ghost. I would really like to meet one.

5. Judy - Well, you've been in Scotland . . . . quite some time now. Don't you have a ghost in your house?

6. Sasha - No, I haven't even heard a mouse . . . .

7. Judy - . . . . , somebody told me that most of the ghosts have left for America. They make a better living over there!

8. Sasha - Oh, that explains it then! I've . . . . thought ghosts were smart. Now I know they definitely are. Is that a ghost I see behind you?

9. Judy - Ahhhhhhh!

SCORE 8

Present perfects • since, for, yet, already • accident words • homonyms

Kathleen's Blog

▸ Complete Kathleen's blog by conjugating the verb in brackets in the present perfect simple, present perfect continuous or simple past.

Edinburgh - Hogmanay 2004
28 Dec 2003 to 1 Jan 2004

For the past eleven years, Edinburgh (1. host).. not just Europe's but possibly the world's most exciting New Year's Eve celebrations. The Scottish New Year is known as Hogmanay. It is a four-day festival of parades, fireworks, concerts, street theatre and general spectacle, all culminating in a huge street party on the night itself in Princes Street, the city's main drag. I (2. die).. to see it for years, but I (3. spend) .... the last several New Year's Eves at home, enviously watching the festivities from Edinburgh on television. However, last year, Jimmy and I (4. decide) .... that in 2003/04 we would go to Scotland.

We (5. line up) .... our accommodation in April 2003. We also (6. arrange) .... to get passes for the New Year's Eve Street Party in Princes Street by becoming members of the First Foot Club, the 'friends' of Edinburgh's Hogmanay. They have a website at: www.edinburghshogmanay.org.

When we (7. arrive) .... we (8. have) .... a late dinner and a good night's sleep. We (9. start)...................................... our sightseeing with Holyroodhouse. The Palace is the Queen's official residence in Scotland and so is very impressive. We (10. visit) .... Mary Queen of Scots' suite of rooms. As she (11. always be) .... a bit of a historical heroine of mine, this was wonderful to see. One room in particular (12. feature) .... a large collection of the effects of Mary which the Royal Family (13. acquire) .... over the years. The room (14. be) .... extensively restored in the 1980s. We were so tired after all the visiting we had done we (15. go) .... and (16. have).. a lie down at the hotel. When we (17. wake up).. it was New Year's day. Hogmanay (18. be) .... over. We had overslept. So, we still (19. not experience) .... a real Scottish New Year. We (20. decide) .... to go back next year. Please join us.

20
SCORE

Accident crossword

Vocabulary to know in case you have an accident climbing Ben Nevis!

DOWN

1. Something that must be dealt with or handled immediately is this.

2. If you hurt yourself you can often be in...

3. If you fall you can do this to your arm or leg.

4. Synonym for 'save'.

5. The doctor gives you this to make sure you are in good health.

6. Synonym for 'to make better'.

7. Someone who takes a lot of useless risks is this.

ACROSS

a. An unexpected and dangerous situation.

b. You use this to cover someone who is cold.

c. This is what you are carried on if you can't walk.

d. If you are ill the doctor gives you some of this to take.

e. If you want people to find you, you must do this so they can hear you.

12
SCORE

Replace coffeepot with the right word.

Each pair of words has exactly the same pronunciation but different spelling.

You must never under a Scotsman's kilt.

1 ....

Ben Nevis is the highest in Scotland.

The English have a reputation for streaking. This involves running across a football pitch.

2 ....

The big brown is an animal which used to live in the Scottish Highlands.

There are large flat, treeless areas of land in Scotland called or moors.

3 ....

There are a lot of flying from Scotland to Europe.

The Scots are a hardworking people. They are definitely not .

4 ....

Annie Lennox is a famous Scottish pop .

Scots a lot of whisky into their Dundee fruitcake mixture.

5 ....

The Scottish cultural heritage is far from being . It is immensely rich.

The Scots considered Mary Stuart to be the rightful to the English throne. But the English recognized Elizabeth.

.... 6 ....

The Scots are considering improving quality by banning smoking in public places.

There are plentiful supplies of to be found in farms along the Scottish coastline. Shellfish is abundant there.

.... 7 ....

Walking in the Highlands will make your leg nice and strong.

Have you of the famous trademark of the Highland Games, tossing the caber?

.... 8 ....

Highland Cattle is the oldest Scottish breed of cow. The Queen has a at Balmoral Castle.

A Scotsman wears a kilt and has a sporran (where he keeps his money) attached to a belt round his .

.... 9 ....

Us Scots are famous for being careful with our money. We do not like to anything.

You are not in the streets of Edinburgh on New Year's Eve unless you buy a special ticket.

.... 10 ....

Scottish poems are much better when they are read . It is wonderful to listen to someone reading Robert Burns' poems.

He an enormous salmon when he went fishing in Scotland.

.... 11 ....

When he was fed up with fishing he played tennis on a beautiful .

SCORE	11

Test yourself on kit 4

Right or wrong?

	right	wrong
1. The PRESENT PERFECT refers to a fixed time in the past: **He's been there last year.**	❑	❑
2. I have lived here since five years.	❑	❑
3. I've been waiting here for ages.	❑	❑
4. Why haven't you called me yesterday to say you weren't coming?	❑	❑
5. He has already been to Scotland.	❑	❑
6. They haven't already visited Edinburgh. But they are definitely going to visit it.	❑	❑
7. Tartan has become one of the the main symbols of Scottish culture.	❑	❑
8. Celts have used striped and checked material since thousands of years.	❑	❑
9. A **MEDICINE** is a doctor.	❑	❑
10. If you **SHOUT** you cry.	❑	❑
11. **HEIR** and **AIR** are pronounced the same.	❑	❑
12. **MUSCLES** are seafood.	❑	❑

12
SCORE

past continuous

is used:

- **when you want to show that while one action is happening another action suddenly happens:**
They were living in Los Angeles when the earthquake struck.

- **when you want to show how you feel about the action that happened in the past:**
It was raining and raining and raining.

Remember the SIMPLE PAST is used to talk about an action WHICH IS COMPLETELY FINISHED:
We left San Francisco and moved to New York last year.

past perfect

is used:

- **to talk about an action which happened before another action in the past:**
New York had already had housing problems before the new wave of immigration started.

make or do?

MAKE is used:

- **to suggest creation, construction, or manufacturing:**
make a house, make a cake, make a plan to do something...

- **or when referring**
to talk and sounds: *make a comment, a noise, a joke, a point...*
to plans: *make arrangements, a decision...*
to journeys: *make a trip*

MAKE can be followed by an object + adjective or object + infinitive:
He made everyone happy. He made everyone feel good.

DO is used:

- **when we don't want to say exactly what it is we're doing:**
The problem was serious and we had to do something but we didn't know what.

- **to talk about activities with words ending in ING + THE:**
I do the shopping and he does the cooking.

Don't forget that DO is also used for the auxiliary in questions and negatives.

Do you have a car ?
You don't need a car in New York City.

past tenses

Whodunnit?

Help Inspector Brown solve the murder mystery. To find out what really happened and in the right sequence of events, circle the right past tense in each sentence.

ILLUSTRATIONS: ANNE DE COURSEULLES

1. Inspector: Mrs. Smith, I'm Inspector Brown, you had called/called/were calling us a few minutes ago. Show me your husband's body.

2. Mrs Smith: This is how I had found/found/was finding him. He had been lying/lied/was lying on the floor.
Inspector: Where had you been/were you being/were you at the time?

3. Mrs Smith: I had slept/slept/was sleeping. He had gone out/went out/was going out to see someone and didn't know when he had come/came/was coming back. I had been/was/was being in bed for at least an hour when this terrible noise woke me up.

4. Inspector: You had slept/slept/were sleeping when you had heard/heard/were hearing the shot?
Mrs Smith: Yes. I got out of bed and ran to the living room. And there he was, on the floor. I knew immediately he had been/was/was being murdered.

5. Inspector: Then what had you done/did you do/were you doing ?
Mrs Smith: I looked for the murderer and couldn't see him in the garden, but the gun was just outside the window. I had picked/picked/was picking it up and brought it inside.

6. Inspector: How did you know that he had been killed/was killed/was being killed by a gun?
Mrs Smith: Well, I.... We've always had a gun in the house, so I just assumed that... There it is, on the floor. I put it next to his body.

7. Inspector: I'm afraid you will have to come with me. I'm charging you with your husband's murder.
Mrs Smith: But you can't. I hadn't done/didn't do/was not doing it.

How does the inspector know she's guilty?

The inspector knows she is guilty because she says her husband and the gun both came in from the outside and yet they're totally dry. It had been raining all day and they ought to have been as wet as the inspector was when he first came in. It's obvious the woman's husband had never been outside. She must have killed him.

past tenses

A Manhattan LOVE STORY

Match the beginning and the end of each sentence to tell this love story between two neighbors in New York City.

1. Before I moved to New York, ...
2. I had decided to move a year ago ....
3. I was afraid of being alone in the big city ....
4. I needed to be in the city ....
5. I had asked friends for names of people to see ....
6. The loneliness was starting to depress me ....
7. She had just settled into the building ....
8. I was coming back from the supermarket ....
9. She was taking letters to the post office ....
10. We had already noticed each other ....
11. Last night we decided to get married ....

a. because things were changing in my professional life.
b. when I met a next-door neighbor.
c. when I saw her in the elevator.
d. I had been living in the country.
e. even though we both had always been against marriage.
f. but this time we spoke.
g. but the ones I called were always busy.
h. before I actually did it.
i. and she wanted to meet new people.
j. and was constantly putting off the big moment.
k. and seemed to be in a hurry.

11

John and Jane arrived in New York City last night. They are planning their day. Choose between MAKE and DO in their conversation.

1. Jane: What do you want to make/do today? Have you made/done any plans for us?

2. John: No. I'm cool. Whatever you got in mind, I'll make/do that too.

3. Jane: Okay. I'd like to walk around the Village and then make/do a museum.

4. John: That sounds good. What did you make/do with the map we bought yesterday?

5. Jane: It's here. Remember you made/did me put it in my bag.

6. John: I'm gonna make/do my best to find us a cute little walk across Chelsea and into the Gramercy Park area.

7. Jane: Nice. Really nice. Can we make/do some shopping in the East Village too?

8. John: Sure. We can even make/do a quick trip to Alphabet City if you want.

9. Jane: Anywhere where it's quiet. The traffic here in midtown makes/does so much noise that it's driving me crazy.

10. John: Don't worry. And don't stress out. That's the worst thing you can make/do. I'll take care of everything and make/do this a day you'll always remember.

11. Jane: All of that sounds perfect. We should also make/do arrangements to go to the theater while we're here.

12. John: That's easily made/done. We can call from the hotel phone and make/do a reservation with our credit card.

15
SCORE

big city words

Brainstorm scramble

All the words below have some connection with the lifestyle of a big city. Unscramble the letters to find the words.

** We've done the first ones for you

Words associated with a big city lifestyle

- ycanf — F a n c Y
- 1. dotcatissiphe — S.................D
- 2. spinveexe — E.................E
- 3. suehrd — R.................D
- 4. slaauc — C.................L
- 5. furtsless — S.................L
- 6. lomicepen — P.................N
- 7. oowwnntd — D.................N
- 8. tencenvion — C.................T
- 9. aabifoslehns — F.................E
- 10. artcfif — T.................C
- 11. urulxy — L.................Y
- 12. dyrnet — T.................Y

SCORE: ___ / 12

Clockword

▸ Use the clue box to help find where the words in the circles begin.

The letters in red all have the 'O' sound as in 'more'.

CLUEBOX
a • no smoothness
b • exceptional
c • state of not being interested
d • no longer married
e • strong and powerful
f • statement of approval or support
g • not now but at a previous time
h • something to tell people about a danger
i • a tape, video, or cd of something
j • significant and essential

9
SCORE

Test yourself on kit 5

Right or wrong?

	right	wrong
1. Mrs Smith was sleeping when she had heard the shot.	❑	❑
2. Had you had any training in the field before you got your first job?	❑	❑
3. They were working hard last year.	❑	❑
4. She had a bath when the murderer strangled her.	❑	❑
5. What were you doing yesterday when I had called you?	❑	❑
6. I am going to do the dishes and then do some shopping.	❑	❑
7. Have you done arrangements for a taxi to come and take us to the airport?	❑	❑
8. What did you make to make him so angry?	❑	❑
9. When something is convenient, it is difficult to do it.	❑	❑
10. If you wear casual clothing, you are very formally dressed.	❑	❑
11. If something is FANCY it is very plain and serious.	❑	❑
12. The vowel sounds of WAR and MORE are the same.	❑	❑

	12
SCORE	

futures

• will (+Verb)

is used to predict the future:
If London goes on charging a fee to drive in the city, the town will get very rich.

is used to express a spontaneous decision in the future:
You look lost. London is such a big city. I'll show you the way.

is used in the question form to ask someone to do something:
You want the taxi cab to stop.
You say: 'Will you please stop here? Thank you.'

• shall (+Verb)

is used less and less in the first person:
It is mainly used in the question form to offer something to someone.
Shall I give you a lift to London? I'm going there too.

• be going to (+Verb)

is used to express an intention based on present facts:
Lots of museums are free in London. We are going to visit them all.
Look at the clouds. I think it's going to rain.

question words

who, what, where, how, when, whose, which, why, how far, how long.

Who did you call? What do you mean? Where are you going?

BE CAREFUL:

• if WHO, WHAT or WHICH are the subject there is no auxiliary:
Who came with you? What happened? Which person spoke to you?

• don't begin a question with a preposition - put the preposition at the end:
Who is she going to stay with?
Which famous house is he going to look at?

• if you begin a question with: 'Do you know... ' or 'Can you tell me....':
Do you know where Charles has gone?
NOT ~~Do you know where has gone Charles?~~

futures

Use one of the verbs to make sentences in the GOING TO future:

take, watch, go up in, buy, see, steal

ILLUSTRATIONS: ANNE DE COURSEULLES

1. He/a cab

. . . .

2. They/the wheel

. . . .

3. They/a match

. . . .

4. She/a travelcard

. . . .

5. They/a show

. . . .

6. He/the bag

. . . .

Complete with will or shall

7. . . . . you come for a walk along the Thames with us?

8. I want some fish'n'chips. . . . . I get you some?

9. . . . . you please be quiet. You are in the British Museum.

9 SCORE

question words

Use these question words to make questions about the words in bold: **how many**, **how old**, **who**, **what** , **when**, **why**, **where**, **how**, **what else**, **how long**.

1. They will cope with growth in London **by increasing bus services.**

. . . .

2. **The government** will increase funding for local transport services.

. . . .

3. There are going to be **800 000** more people living in London in the next decade.

. . . .

4. **630 000 jobs** will **also** be created in the same period.

. . . .

5. We are going to buy **a travel card** to get round London while we are there...

. . . .

6. ... because a travel card is **the cheapest way of getting around**.

. . . .

7. We are going to visit Buckingham Palace **tomorrow.**

. . . .

8. It's only going to take about **two and a half hours** to get from London to Paris by train in the near future.

. . . .

9. We will be coming from **the North of London**.

. . . .

10. The Tower of London is **over 800 years old**.

. . . .

	10
SCORE	

urban words

Find the first word and transform it into the second word which has something to do with the urban environment.

1. It is blue and over our heads.	Buildings that tower over our heads.
2. A prefix which means under.	An area of the town far from the centre.
3. A shop.	A floor in a building.
4. Succeed in an exam.	A pedestrian.
5. Cover with concrete.	A sidewalk.
6. The tube inside the abdomen.	Edge of the road where water drains off.
7. A type of medicine you take with water.	A place to post your letters.
8. Money.	A hole in the wall to get money out of.
9. A pattern of lines that cross over each other.	When there is a traffic jam.
10. A large deep cup with straight sides	Robbery in towns.

10
SCORE

Match what we hear to what is really said

1. I'm gonna go.
2. I gotta go.
3. I wanna go.
4. Djew go?
5. Djew go?
6. I wunnagone.
7. Watta you want?
8. Watdja want?
9. I shunna come.
10. I shudda come.

a. I have got to go.
b. Did you go?
c. What did you want?
d. I am going to go.
e. Do you go?
f. I should have come.
g. What do you want?
h. I should not have come.
i. I want to go.
j. I would not have gone.

1. ....
2. ....
3. ....
4. ....
5. ....
6. ....
7. ....
8. ....
9. ....
10. ....

| 10 |
| SCORE |

Test yourself on kit 6

Right or wrong?

	right	wrong
1. WILL is used to talk about a future plan.	❑	❑
2. Your bag looks heavy. Will I help you?	❑	❑
3. Shall you come tonight?	❑	❑
4. Shall you please stop talking?	❑	❑
5. What are you going to do tomorrow in London?	❑	❑
6. When you think are you going to see him?	❑	❑
7. From where are you coming?	❑	❑
8. Since how long have you been waiting here?	❑	❑
9. GRIDLOCK is a synonym of a TRAFFIC JAM.	❑	❑
10. STOREY is a synonym of TALE.	❑	❑
11. GONNA is an assimilation of GOT TO.	❑	❑
12. DJEW can mean both DID YOU and DO YOU.	❑	❑

12
SCORE

conditionals

To talk about a situation that might possibly happen and say what its results might be, you use the conditionals in the following ways:

- **to express possibility or a general rule:** *If it rains, I won't go. If you like kangaroos, you can go to Australia to see them live.*
  Never put WILL after IF
  If I ~~will~~ call
- **to express a possible but improbable condition:** *If I lived in Sydney, I would go surfing on the beach every day.* It's possible but not very probable for me to live in Sydney.
- **to express impossibility or a missed chance:** *If I had been born an Aboriginal, I would have learned to use a boomerang.* Here, the condition is impossible. I am not and cannot become an Aboriginal.
- **to indicate that one thing only happens or is true if another situation happens or is true:** *I'll come tomorrow only if you're sure to be there.*

Sometimes the conditional is created without an 'if' clause to express something exceptional :
as long as, only if, provided, provided that
I will do what you want provided you pay for everything.

comparatives & superlatives

Short adjectives	The idea of 'more': adjective **+ er + than**: *Sydney is bigger than Melbourne.*	The idea of 'most': **the +** adjective **+ est**: *Sydney is the richest city.*
Long adjectives	**more +** adjective **+ than**: *Australian beaches are more natural than European ones.*	**the most +** adjective: *Tazmania is the most fascinating island of all.*
Nouns, verbs, or adverbs	**More + than**: *I work more than I did three years ago.*	
Adverbs and adjectives	The idea of 'less': **Not as +** adv/adj **+ than**: *That restaurant is not as good as this one.* **Less +** adv/adj **+ than**: *That car costs less than mine.*	The idea of 'least': **the least +** adjective: *This is the least expensive item we have.*
Adverbs and adjectives	The idea of 'equal': **As +** adv/adj **+ as**: *He ran as fast as I did. My computer is as good as yours.*	**irregular comparatives and superlatives:** • good, better, the best • bad, worse, the worst • old, elder, the eldest

conditionals

Two people are standing in front of **Uluru**. Keith is from Sydney, Sarah is an Aboriginal living near the rock.

1. Sarah: Welcome here. As long as . . . the rules of our national park, I can take you to certain parts of the park.
- ❑ you obey
- ❑ you obeyed
- ❑ you have obeyed

2. Keith: Thank you. If . . . how beautiful the rock was, I would have come here earlier.
- ❑ I know
- ❑ I had known
- ❑ I knew

3. S: Let's start our walk. . . . a hat if I were you. The sun can be very strong.
- ❑ I had taken
- ❑ I would take
- ❑ I take

4. K: Okay, if you give me a minute, . . . one in this little shop.
- ❑ I would try and find
- ❑ I would have tried and find
- ❑ I'll try and find

5. S: So off we go. First of all, if I asked you what you know about 'The Dreaming', what . . . ?
- ❑ were you saying?
- ❑ would you say?
- ❑ did you say?

6. K: I know that it is an Aboriginal word for the beginning of the world, but if you . . . please tell me more.
- ❑ don't mind
- ❑ hadn't minded
- ❑ wouldn't have minded

7. S: A long, long time ago, ancient heroes, resembling plants or animals, wandered through the land. If you had been alive then, you . . . like them.
- ❑ would have been
- ❑ would be
- ❑ had been

K: How did they create th world?

8. S: If they . . . the world it would have remained i its formless state.
- ❑ wouldn't shape
- ❑ hadn't shaped
- ❑ haven't shaped

9. K: So if I . . . something today, it means it was shape by the ancient heroes.
- ❑ see
- ❑ saw
- ❑ had seen

10. S: That's right. If you want to understand today' world, you . . . to know about 'The Dreaming'.
- ❑ had
- ❑ have had
- ❑ have

SCORE ___ / 10

You've just come back from Australia.

You want to give your impressions.
Pick the right way to say what you think about your trip.

1. Kangaroos are ... many other animals.
a. ❑ **more exotic than**
b. ❑ **most exotic as**
c. ❑ **as exoticker as**

2. Kaola bears are ... of all.
a. ❑ **as most cuter animals**
b. ❑ **most cutest animals**
c. ❑ **the cutest animals**

3. The Australian beaches are ... for surfing in all the South Pacific.
a. ❑ **the best**
b. ❑ **the most better**
c. ❑ **the bestest**

4. Eucalyptus trees are ... that I know.
a. ❑ **the aromaticest**
b. ❑ **the most aromatic**
c. ❑ **the best aromatic**

5. The didgeridoo is a musical instrument which makes ... most other instruments.
a. ❑ **most harmonious sounds than**
b. ❑ **harmoniouser sounds as**
c. ❑ **more harmonious sounds than**

6. I found the Sydney Opera House ... I thought it was going to be.
a. ❑ **not so ugly than**
b. ❑ **not as ugly as**
c. ❑ **not least as ugly than**

7. A lot of Australian wines taste ... many European wines.
a. ❑ **better than**
b. ❑ **more better than**
c. ❑ **better as**

8. The Aboriginals' way of life is ... to nature.
a. ❑ **more close**
b. ❑ **closer as**
c. ❑ **closer**

9. Australian English is ... British or American English.
a. ❑ **as difficult as**
b. ❑ **than difficult as**
c. ❑ **as difficult than**

10. Australian food is, I'm sorry to say, ... French food.
a. ❑ **the least appealing than**
b. ❑ **less appealing than**
c. ❑ **as less appealing than**

10
SCORE

compound words

Word builders ▸ Use the word in the center to build compound words.

We've given you a definition and sometimes the first letter for each word. Use the words in the box to build your compound words.

dead	less	out	un
hand	less	proof	up
ing	loader	result	way
lance	mate	track	point

check

- A place to control people and vehicles: check p o i n t
- A winning chess move: check m _ _ _
- A medical exam: check-u _
- Where you pay in supermarkets: check o _ _

sound

- Sealed against noise: sound p _ _ _ _
- Quiet or without any noise: sound l _ _ _
- The music of a movie: sound t _ _ _ _
- Not very certain or reliable: _ _ sound

end

- What you get after a long process or work: end-r _ _ _ _ _
- The last part of a book, story, play or film: end _ _ _
- A street that leads nowhere: d _ _ _ -end
- Unlimited or continuous: end _ _ _

free

- Someone who takes advantages of others' generosity: free l _ _ _ _ _
- A road: free w _ _
- A way to draw: free h _ _ _
- Self-employed: free l _ _ _ _

SCORE: ___ / 15

late
sound puzzle

Use the definitions to find the words below. Each answer contains the vowel sound of 'late' in the word.

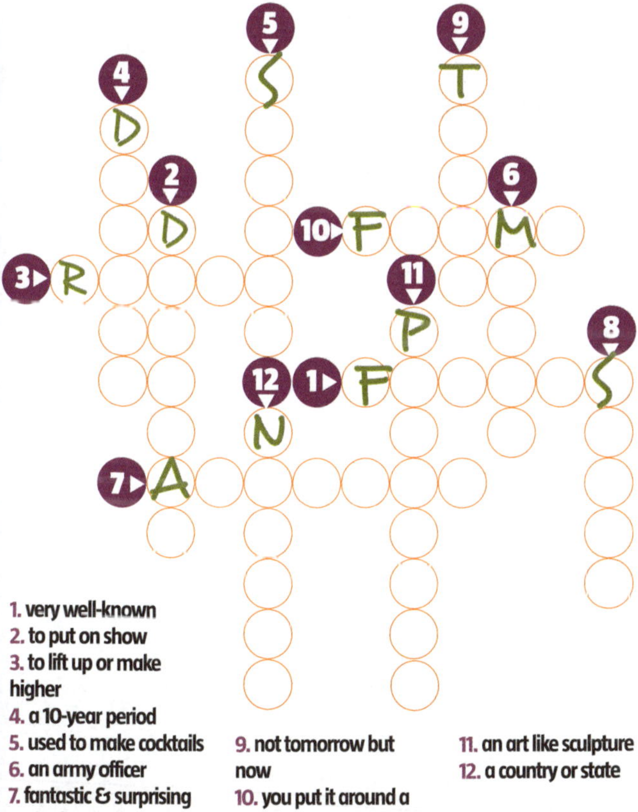

1. very well-known
2. to put on show
3. to lift up or make higher
4. a 10-year period
5. used to make cocktails
6. an army officer
7. fantastic & surprising
8. the floor in a theatre
9. not tomorrow but now
10. you put it around a picture
11. an art like sculpture
12. a country or state

	12
SCORE	

Test yourself on kit 7

Right or wrong?

	right	wrong
1. You can never use will in the conditional.	❑	❑
2. When you want to express the idea of something being impossible, you use this conditional: **If I lived in New York, I would be happy.**	❑	❑
3. If I had had the time, I would have had the money too.	❑	❑
4. If it will rain, I would take an umbrella.	❑	❑
5. I'll help you as long as you need me.	❑	❑
6. Australia is as fascinating than New Zealand.	❑	❑
7. Ostrich meat is not as bad as I thought.	❑	❑
8. Some European wines are worser than some Australian ones.	❑	❑
9. Something that you find stupid, you call MINDFUL.	❑	❑
10. The words GREAT and EIGHT do not have the same vowel sound.	❑	❑

SCORE: /10

EMERGENCY GRAMMAR Kit 8

can, could

permission
Can I use your computer, please? Could I use your computer? (more polite)

interdiction
You can't use my computer. Use your own.

ability
He can speak English and French. He could speak French when he was young. (he can't today)

general facts
You can fly to Canada very cheaply on a no-frills airline.

CAN in the future: *You will be able to go next year.*

must, may, could, might, can't

refer to the **possibility** of something happening:
We must/may/could/might/can't go.

ALMOST SURE >>>> NOT SURE AT ALL

MUST	MAY	COULD	MIGHT	CAN'T
100%	50%	40%	30%	0%

must, have to

You mustn't go = interdiction
You don't have to go/You haven't got to go = You are not being forced to go.

should=ought to

should/ought to = advice
You should/ought to visit Prince Edward Island. It is beautiful.

prepositions of time

AT for a precise time:
at five o'clock, at the weekend, at Christmas, at Easter...

IN for a period of time:
in the morning, in the evening, in 1987, in the 1970s...

ON for a precise date:
on the 16th of August, on Monday...

FIRST = for a list of things:
First, we went to the zoo, then we had lunch.

AT FIRST = at the beginning (and then later the situation changed):
At first he was polite, then he became rude.

BY = before a precise time
WITHIN = before a length of time
By six o'clock / Within 4 hours

AFTER, BEFORE, DURING, FOR, OVER, SINCE, UNTIL...

can, must, should

Choose the best modal

1. ***Frank:*** How **can/must** I get more information about what to see in Canada?
2. ***Kirsty:*** You **can/might** visit www.travelcanada.com. It is wonderful and really useful.
3. You will **can/be able to** choose the territory you want to visit.

4. ***Frank:*** What **can/may** I see on the site?
5. ***Kirsty:*** Lots of great stuff. You **are able to/must** take the virtual tour, it's unbelievable.

6. ***Frank:*** It **might/must** be cold in winter.
7. ***Kirsty:*** It definitely is. But if you go there in winter you **could/mustn't** go skiing. You **can/might** prefer rafting in summer. If you decide to go on a rafting holiday you **must/can** be fit. Of course, you **don't have to/mustn't** raft all the time. You **could/should** do a bit of bungee jumping too.

8. ***Frank:*** I **couldn't/mustn't** possibly do bungee jumping. I'm such a coward. I **can't/shouldn't** do any dangerous sports. I'm not brave enough.
9. ***Kirsty:*** If you **can't/mustn't** bungee jump you **mustn't/don't have to** do it. There are plenty of other activities you **may/can** do.

10. ***Frank:*** **May/Can** you give me the address again, please? I **might/can** check it out, but I'm not promising I'll go there.
11. ***Kirsty:*** You **can/should** always send me a postcard from the website. Like that I **might /should** even think you took my advice.

20
SCORE

Badlands, Canada

The Dinosaur capital of the world

▸ Complete these sentences about the timeline using these prepositions of time:
during, since, at, before, for, after, within, from, in, on, until

Timeline

75 million years ago	*Dinosaurs lived on earth*
65 million years ago	*Dinosaurs became extinct*
8000 years ago	*Prehistoric man lived here*
1884	*Albertosaurus was found*
June 26th, 1955	*Dinosaur Provincial Park opened*
1987	*Royal Tyrrell museum opened & established summer hours: 9 a.m. to 9 p.m.*
2000	*Finished building largest dinosaur in the world in Drumheller*

1. .... 75 million years of living in the Badlands the dinosaurs disappeared.
2. No one found any remains .... 1884.
3. The Royal Tyrrell Dinosaur museum opens .... 9 a.m. .... summer.
4. .... June 26th,1955 the Dinosaur Provincial Park was opened.
5. .... prehistoric times there were no longer any dinosaurs around.
6. The Museum has been open .... 1987.
7. The giant dinosaur in Drumheller has existed .... four years only.
8. .... 1987 there wasn't any Dinosaur museum in Canada.
9. The museum is open .... 9 a.m. to 9 p.m. in summer.
10. 75 million years ago there were dinosaurs on earth. .... 10 million years they had disappeared.

11 SCORE

weather words

Match the weather to the picture

ILLUSTRATIONS: ANNE DE COURSEULLES

1. freezing ...
2. drizzly ...
3. cloudy ...
4. windy ...
5. stormy ...
6. showers ...
7. black ice ...
8. pouring ...
9. lightning ...
10. thunder ...

SCORE ... / 10

Ve ry ca na di an

● • • ● • •

▸ Match each word to its stress pattern

Toronto	● • • ●
beaver	● • •
maple leaf	● •
Mounted Police	● •
Eskimos	• ● •
Aboriginals	● •
Inuits	● ● • ●
Freezing	● • ●
Two million lakes	● • •
Grizzly bears	• • ● • •

10
SCORE

Test yourself on kit 8

Right or wrong?

	right	wrong
1. Canadians can to speak French really well.	❑	❑
2. **She could ski when she was three** is the same as **she knew how to ski when she was three.**	❑	❑
3. The future of **can** is **will can.**	❑	❑
4. When you say you might do something it is more certain than you may do something.	❑	❑
5. **You don't have to go** means the same as **you mustn't go.**	❑	❑
6. **Should** is slightly stronger than **ought to.**	❑	❑
7. He does not go to work on the Monday. It's his day off.	❑	❑
8. At first I'd like to talk about the Canadian weather.	❑	❑
9. If the weather is drizzly it's pouring with rain.	❑	❑
10. The first syllable of **POLICE** is the stressed syllable.	❑	❑

/ 10
SCORE

Verb + to + Verb

- **often refers to the future**

Nelson Mandela stopped to shake hands with the people.

Compare with: *He stopped shaking hands with people* = this means he never shook hands with people again!

- **often used after verbs expressing a decision**

He chose to lead the country peacefully.

He decided to forgive the whites.

He agreed to run for President.

- **make, let, have + V**

The government eventually let Mandela leave prison.

He made the people love him.

He had the country organise a truth and reconciliation commission.

Verb + Verb-ing

- **often refers to an action that has already started**

The whites stopped governing South Africa when Mandela came to power.

- **after certain verbs and expressions which often explain feelings: feel like, hate, enjoy, worth, can't help, can't stand, give up, look forward to, be/get used to**

It's worth visiting South Africa both for the people and the countryside.

I feel like going on a Safari.

prepositions of place

The red circle is ..... the box(es)

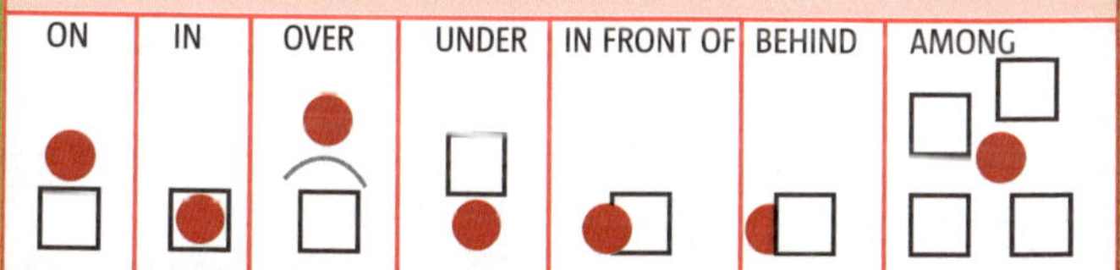

The red circle is moving..... the box(es)

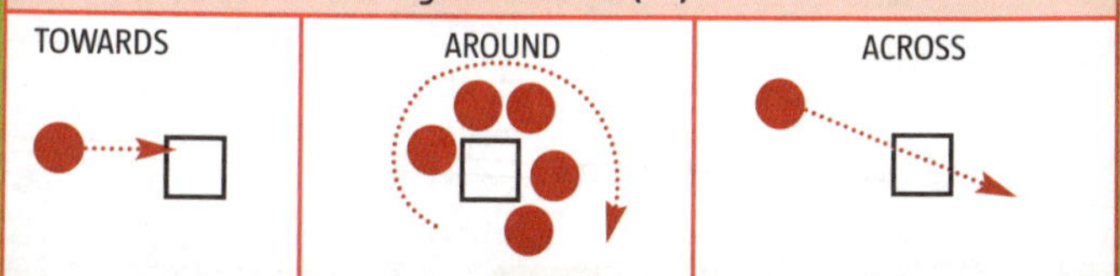

verb+to+V • verb+V-ing

Circle the right verb form

1. Nelson Mandela was prohibited to attend/from attending gatherings.

2. He was convicted to contravene/of contravening the Suppression of Communism Act.

3. Nelson Mandela was forced to go /going to Robben Island.

4. This prison had been used to house /housing lepers.

5. Mandela was not used to live/to living in such a place.

6. He was prevented to see/from seeing his family and friends.

7. South Africans asked the government to release/releasing him.

8. He spent 27 years to live/living in a tiny room.

9. Prisoners were allowed to have /having visitors two or three times a year and all conversations were taped.

10. Today's leaders were created here and they promised to change /changing how their country was run.

11. He agreed to accept /accepting the Nobel Peace Prize as an accolade to everyone who had worked for peace.

12. He especially thanked Norway to help /for helping his country.

13. In January, 1997, Robben Island decided to open/opening its doors to the public as a national monument and museum.

14. All of the tour guides are former political prisoners who hope to open /opening the visitors' eyes to what life used to be like.

14
SCORE

Find the diamonds

▸ Use the right prepositions to say where they are.

- under
- in
- near
- over
- behind
- among
- towards
- on
- around
- in front of
- across

7. Diamond 7 is on the lamp .... the table.

11. Diamond 11 is flying .... the room.

10. The man is throwing Diamond 10 .... the box on the table.

3. Diamond 3 is .... the box.

2. Diamond 2 is .... the box.

1. Diamond 1 is............ the table.

6. Diamond 6 is .... the table.

5. Diamond 5 is .... the leg of the table.

9. Diamond 9 is .... the emeralds and rubies.

4. Diamond 4 is .... Diamond 2.

8. Diamonds 8 are .... the table leg.

11
SCORE

South African words

Some words are specific to South Africa.

South Africans often use the same words as in English-English rather than American-English.

▶ Find the equivalent to the words in purple.

1. You must stop when the **robot** is red. If not you'll get a ticket.
2. He drank so much last night he has a terrible **babbelas** this morning!.
3. He **gave me a bell** last night. He woke me up.
4. Put all those bricks in my **bakkie**. I'll drive it round to your place tonight.
5. Don't panic; I'll be there **now now**.
6. Put your luggage in the **boot** of my car.
7. My car won't start. I'll have to have a look under the **bonnet**.
8. Can you give me a lift? It is such a **trek** to the shops.
9. I think it's about time you **flogged** your car. It is so old.
10. When is **dinges** coming? I can never remember what he's called.

- call me on the phone
- hangover
- hood
- long difficult walk
- pickup truck
- shortly
- sold
- thingamajig
- traffic light
- trunk

	10

SCORE

Opposites
sound puzzle

Find the opposites of the words below. They all have the vowel sound of "wow".

1. country
2. up
3. when there is no one
4. valley
5. lost
6. shaky, unreliable
7. humble
8. flood
9. smile
10. apartment
11. quiet
12. square

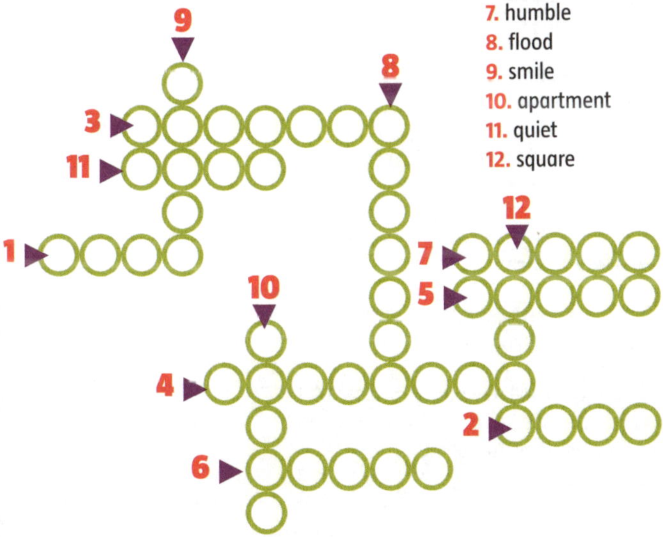

	12
SCORE	

Test yourself on kit 9

Right or wrong?

	right	wrong
1. It's worth to go on a safari. It's a wonderful experience.	❑	❑
2. I wanted that he took me to South Africa with him.	❑	❑
3. He can't stop talking about his journey there.	❑	❑
4. **He stopped to wave** means **he stopped in order to wave.**	❑	❑
5. I'm looking forward to hear from you.	❑	❑
6. **He stopped waving** means **he didn't wave anymore.**	❑	❑
7. The preposition **TOWARDS** means **to move in the direction of.**	❑	❑
8. If Mandela **moves among** the people **he is not close to them.**	❑	❑
9. You get a **HANGOVER** or a **FINE** when the police stop you for speeding.	❑	❑
10. You can use the word **THINGAMAJIG** to refer to a person or object when you don't know what they are called.	❑	❑

	10
SCORE	

Adverbs

Place in the sentence

Adverbs change their position in the sentence according to their meaning.

Adverbs of frequency:

If the adverb answers the question "HOW OFTEN" we call it an adverb of frequency.

- You put it in front of the verb, except with the verb "to be":

He always does his job.

He is always late. (the adverb of frequency is placed after the verb "to be")

- Put the adverb in front of the verb even if there's an auxiliary:

He has always done his job.

Other adverbs :

For all other adverbs, put them after the verb. If there is an object, put the adverb after the object.

He came quickly. He speaks English very well.

not : ~~*He speaks very well English.*~~

Types of adverbs

Adverbs of frequency:

Often, always, usually, never, sometimes, generally, frequently...

Common adverbs of manner:

Quickly, fast, carefully, easily, loudly, quietly, slowly...

Negative adverbs

The following adverbs have a negative meaning: hardly, never, barely, rarely, scarcely, seldom, nowhere...

When you use them in a sentence, do not use a second negative word with the verb.

Example: *He rarely speaks French* or *He doesn't speak French very often.*

adverbs

Burning city

Do you know Burning City in Nevada? The City that only lasts one week!

Put the adverbs in the right place in the sentences below.

1. Many people come to take part in Burning City. • frequently

2. They build the city very, in under two or three days. • quickly

3. They use wood and simple materials to make the buildings. • usually

4. Each person creates his contribution very and some are designed. • carefully

5. Money is not allowed so people give each other food. • freely

6. The atmosphere is very friendly and you can speak to people. • easily

7. Many people come with strange and funny cars that they build to show at Burning City. • specially

8. These vehicles are good examples of how a car doesn't have to pollute the air. • sometimes

9. The Nevada desert is a good place to erect Burning City because it's so quiet and pure. • clearly

10. Tourists don't know about Burning City so it hasn't been spoiled yet. • generally

11. At the end of the week, they burn everything, including the buildings. • always

12. On the last day, you can see everything turning into ashes. • slowly

12

Adverbs or adjectives?

Choose the right expression.

1. When I got to Las Vegas, I went **direct/directly** to the Casino.
2. The man at the roulette wheel spoke to me **very friendly/in a very friendly way**.
3. But I started losing money **too fast/too fastly**.
4. So I decided to take it **easy/easily** and have lunch.
5. Everywhere I could hear people winning money **easy/easily**.
6. But it's not true. You have to try **hard/hardly** to win at Las Vegas.
7. I wanted to win a lot of money and could **hard/hardly** wait to get to the slot machines.
8. At the bar, a woman was playing the piano. **She played lovely/Her playing was lovely.**
9. After an hour or so, I started losing money **slow and sure/slowly and surely**.
10. I made up my mind to go, but I must say I had a **real/really** good time.

DIY words

DIY WORDS for those who like to make things

Unscramble the words to complete the sentences.

1. You use this to hit a nail.
.... M R E H M A

2. You use this when you don't want to use a nail.
.... W R S E C

3. You use this with number 2 to make it enter the wood.
.... S R R D W I R V E C E

4. You use this to cut wood.
.... W A S

5. You use this to make a hole.
.... I L D R L

6. You use this to paint the wood.
.... S U R B H

7. You use this to make the wood smooth and flat.
.... A L N E P

8. You use this to hold two pieces of wood together when you glue them.
.... P M C L A

9. You use these to cut paper or cloth.
.... S S I R O C S S

	9

SCORE

Same but totally different

These words have the same spelling but different pronunciations. Can you find the right meanings for each pronunciation?

wind (as in sit) ....
wind (as in five) ....

tear (as in air) ....
tear (as in beer) ....

deSERT ....
DEsert ....

lead (as in feed) ....
lead (as in bed) ....

polish (as in so) ....
polish (as in pop) ....

PRESent ....
preSENT ....

bow (as in so) ....
bow (as in cow) ....

CONcert ....
conCERT ....

close (s like a z) ....
close (s like ss) ....

row (as in so) ....
row (as in cow) ....

- To turn a rope around something
- To be at the head of a group
- To make the boat go forward with oars
- To work with other people to get their agreement
- To shut down something
- To give some information to other people
- What you use with arrows
- A musical evening
- People from Poland
- Very near
- An argument
- A heavy metal
- To rip
- What you have in your eye when you cry
- A gift
- Air that blows very hard
- To abandon
- To rub and make shine
- A place like the Sahara
- To bend very low

20
SCORE

Test yourself on kit 10

Right or wrong?

	right	wrong
1. You can put any adverb in front of the verb "to be".	❑	❑
2. You put adverbs of manner in front of all verbs.	❑	❑
3. You put adverbs of frequency in front of all verbs except the verb "to be".	❑	❑
4. I make never mistakes in English.	❑	❑
5. He understood everything very fastly.	❑	❑
6. She has always done the job well.	❑	❑
7. I don't hardly know him.	❑	❑
8. You use a screwdriver with nails.	❑	❑
9. You cut wood with a DRILL.	❑	❑
10. The verb "to **lead**" has the same vowel sound as **bed**, and "**lead**" (the heavy metal) has the same vowel sound as **tea**.	❑	❑

	10
SCORE	

Reported speech

When you report what someone says, you must change the sentence accordingly. **If the INTRODUCTORY VERB is in the past you must put what the person says in the past.**

	DIRECT SPEECH	REPORTED SPEECH
• Present → simple past	*He says: "Ireland **is** a wonderful country."*	*He said Ireland **was** a wonderful country.*
• Simple Past → past perfect	*He says: "I **visited** Ireland last year."*	*He said he **had visited** Ireland last year.*
Sometimes we don't use the past perfect, just the past, it depends on the situation.		
• Present perfect → past perfect	*He says: "I **have** never **seen** such a green country."*	*He said he **had** never **seen** such a green country.*
(present perfect continuous → past perfect continuous)		
• Past perfect → Past perfect	*He says: "I **had** never **been** to Ireland before".*	*He said he **had** never **been** to Ireland before.*
• Future in will → would	*He says: "I'**ll** go there next year."*	*He said he **would** go there next year.*

Time words

These words must often be put in the past too:

- Now → then
- Today → that day
- Tomorrow → the next day
- Yesterday → the day before
- This week → the following week
- Here → there

etc.

Reporting questions

- **Use these verbs:** ASK, WONDER, WANT TO KNOW

He asked me: "When did you go to Ireland?"
→ He asked me when I had been to Ireland.

- **If there is no question word use** IF:

"Have you been to Ireland before?" he asked.
→ He asked me if I had been to Ireland before.

Reporting orders

Use these verbs: TELL, ORDER, FORBID, ASK, ADVISE
He said: "You must go there."
→ He told us we had to go there.

Say or Tell

You tell someone something.
You say something to someone.

reported speech

The Celtic Tiger

Report this interview between a journalist and an economist. Use the verbs in brackets to report the questions.

We've done the first one for you

Journalist - What is Ireland like today? (*ask*)

The journalist asked what Ireland was like today.

Economist - Would you be surprised if I were to say it was now the world's biggest exporter of computer software? (*reply*)

The economist replied by asking the journalist if he would be surprised if he were to say that it was now the world's biggest exporter of computer software.

1. J - Of course I would. How fast has this change been? (*reply, wonder*)

....

....

2. E - Well, ten years ago, Ireland was reputed for its slow pace of life and high unemployment. Today, the Irish economy is booming. (*answer, continue by saying*)

....

....

....

....

....

3. J - So, what happened? (*want to know*)

....

4. E - In a few words, the situation can be explained by economic liberalism and low taxes. (*say*)

....

....

....

....

5. J - How is the economy doing at the moment? (*go on to ask*)

....

....

6. E - Today, the Irish economy is the fastest growing in Europe. (*reply*)

....

....

....

7. J - I thought transport was very bad. (*say*)

....

....

8. E - Thanks to information superhighways distance from the rest of Europe has been abolished. (*reply*)

....

....

....

....

reported speech

9. J - Tell us about Dublin. (*ask*)

....

....

10. E - Dublin has become one of the main cosmopolitan cities of Europe. (*say*)

....

....

....

....

11. J - Has everything gone easily, without any hitches? (*wonder*)

....

....

12. E - Naturally, all this has not come without problems; the vast influx of capital and people has put enormous pressures on the country's infrastructures, particularly in Dublin. (*explain*)

....

....

....

....

....

13. J - So, are the Irish regretting this sudden growth? (*want to know*)

....

....

14. E - You must be kidding. After centuries of being on the fringe of Europe, Ireland is now at the centre. The Celtic Tiger looks set to keep roaring for many years to come. (*tell, add, say*)

....

....

....

....

....

17
SCORE

reported speech

The dolphin of Dingle Bay

Write the dialogue by converting the reported speech into direct speech. Use correct punctuation.

We've done the first one for you

One day Paddy Ferriter said he could see a lone wild dolphin in the sea.

Paddy said: "I can see a lone, wild dolphin in the sea."

1. He told his fellow worker to look at the dolphin.

2. He was escorting the town's fishing boats to and from port.

3. Marine Manager, Kevin Flannery said he was going to officially record the dolphin as a "permanent" resident of Dingle Bay.

4. Paddy told the tourists the dolphin had developed into a playful, though mischievous, companion.

5. A child asked him the dolphin's name.

6. Paddy said it was Fungie.

7. One tourist asked him if Fungie was a social outcast.

8. Paddy replied that he wasn't. He explained he often met other dolphins and porpoises.

9. He explained that thousands of visitors had been coming to Dingle Bay ever since Fungie had arrived. He hoped it would continue.

9 SCORE

Say or Tell

Quinn and his family emigrated to the USA twenty years ago. He has decided to come home to Ireland. Complete his conversation with his mum using SAY or TELL conjugated accordingly.

1. **Mum** - Hallo, Quinn. How are you and the family? How is little Eamon? Can he .... the time yet?

2. **Quinn** - Yes he can, mum. You will be seeing him very soon. I have some good news to .... you.

3. **Mum** - You have, dear. What is it? .... me quickly.

4. **Quinn** - We are moving back to Ireland. What do you .... to that?

5. **Mum** - What? Did you .... you were coming home?

6. **Quinn** - Yes, I did. And I am not .... lies. It is true.

7. **Mum** - I am so happy. I .... you, you wouldn't be happy in America!

8. **Quinn** - We were happy, mum. But, how can I .... , we want Eamon to see where he comes from. I've also been offered a computer job in Dublin. My boss .... it's hard to .... the difference between Silicon Valley and Dublin today.

9. **Mum** - Needless to .... , there is a big difference. Dublin is far better. I have a wonderful joke to .... you: an American tourist was boasting to an Irishman how advanced the Americans are. "Gee, we've even put a man on the moon." "That's nothing," replied the Irishman, "we're going to put a man on the sun." "Don't be stupid," .... the American," "he'll fry before he even gets there." "Oh no, he won't. We're sending him at night."

10. **Quinn** - Oh, mum, you haven't changed! See you next week. Don't forget to .... dad.

	14
SCORE	

computer words

COMPUTER WORDS

▶ Match each computer word to its meaning.

1. bookmark
2. browser
3. click
4. delete
5. download
6. highlight
7. keyboard
8. link
9. log on
10. trial
11. troubleshoot
12. update
13. upgrade

a • a connection to another page
b • a favourite web address
c • a test product
d • an application used to visit web-sites
e • connect onto a computer with your password
f • emphasize something with a bright colour
g • find out what the problems are
h • improve quality
i • press and release a button on your mouse
j • provide recent information
k • remove or erase information
l • transfer data from one computer to another
m • used to type on

13 SCORE

Pronouncing vowel sounds

Complete these Irish proverbs with the right word from the word box below.

break • day • light • says • mouth • never • silent • seldom • lie • house • praise • how

The missing word contains the "e" sound as in "bed".

1. A diplomat must always think twice before he ....nothing.
2. A dog owns nothing, yet is ....dissatisfied.
3. A turkey ....voted for an early Christmas.

The missing word contains the "i" sound as in "five".

4. A ....travels farther than the truth.
5. A ....heart lives long.
6. A ....mouth is sweet to hear.

The missing word contains the "ow" sound as in "cow".

7. Bricks and mortar make a ...., but the laughter of children makes a home.
8. You've got to do your own growing, no matter ....tall your grandfather was.
9. A kind word never broke anyone's ....

The missing word contains the "a" sound as in "way".

10. Don't ....your shin on a stool that is not in your way.
11. Even the longest ....has its end.
12. ....youth and it will prosper.

12 SCORE

Test yourself on kit 11

Right or wrong?

	right	wrong
1. He asked what is Ireland like today.	❑	❑
2. If a sentence is in the simple past when somebody speaks, you have to put it into the past perfect to report it.	❑	❑
3. He asked the Irish economy was booming.	❑	❑
4. The past of MUST is HAD TO.	❑	❑
5. He advised people go to Ireland for their holidays.	❑	❑
6. My kid knows how to say the time.	❑	❑
7. My mum loves saying jokes.	❑	❑
8. He told he was happy.	❑	❑
9. If you upgrade your computer you change the date in it.	❑	❑
10. The red vowels in head and bed are pronounced the same.	❑	❑

10 SCORE

Making the passive

The passive is: **"be"** in all its forms (am/is/was/were/have been/will be/would be, etc.) + **the past participle** (done/seen/made, etc.).
It was done yesterday.

Using the passive

• **when who or what causes the action is often unknown or unimportant:**
My house was robbed during the holidays. = Somebody robbed my house.

• **when writing reports or describing procedures or processes:**
Good service isn't being given. = People don't give good service.

• **when a subject contains a lot of information**:
compare : *I was surprised by the bad service I got. / The bad service I got surprised me.*

• **when you want to report what was said by someone, the passive is very useful:**
I was told the swimming pool was going to be cleaned quickly. = They told me they were going to clean the swimming pool quickly.

The passive tenses

• **Simple present : constant facts or generalizations.** *Senior citizens are well cared for in Florida.*

• **Present continuous: temporary situations or events happening now .**
Your hotel room is being prepared right now.

• **Present perfect: when the action began in the past and continues into the present or if the result is more important than the action.**
These places in the Everglades have been selected because they are interesting to see.

• **Simple past : when the action is finished and/or when there is a specific time or date:**
These palm trees were planted last year.

• **Past perfect: the action happened before the past.**
Miami hadn't been chosen by many people before my parents moved there.

• **Past continuous : temporary situation in the past.**
The beaches were being used only by fishermen when we first came to Miami.

• **Conditional : when events that are possible but not probable, or to replace "will" in reported speech :**
Smoking would be banned if people realized the dangers of tobacco.

• **Past conditional : to say that something is "too late" or impossible.**
This travel guide could have been written by a monkey, it's so stupid.

the passive

Use the passive to visit Key West

Put the verbs in the right passive PRESENT tense.

1. We (take) .... on a trip today to see Key West.
2. It (know) .... to be a famous place for artists and writers.
3. Diving and snorkeling (make) .... into very popular tourists activities too.
4. On some cruises champagne (offer) .... at the end of the day.
5. On some boat rides dolphins (can see) .... jumping in water.
6. Special glass boats (build) .... so you can see underwater.
7. The departure point (locate) .... at the end of the dock.
8. Coral reefs (include) .... as part of the trip.
9. They are fragile and (constantly damage) .... by tourists.
10. Let's go on board the boat now. Cocktails (serve) .... just before lunch.
11. This boat trip (organize) .... very well. I really am enjoying it.

SCORE 11

Mixed present and past passives

Choose the right passive tense.

Listen to what John says about his trip to the Kennedy Space Center.

1. It was great! You .... welcomed by a team from NASA.

2. I .... given the choice of an ordinary tour or the ATX, Astronaut Training Experience. I chose the ATX.

3. It's expensive. You'll .... made to pay $225 for the day.

4. But it's worth it. First, you .... taken on an exclusive guided tour of the Space Center.

5. Then you .... briefed by a NASA Astronaut before beginning the training program.

6. Once you .... fitted out in exclusive ATX equipment and served a freshly prepared Astronaut meal, you are ready to go.

7. I .... put inside a model of a full-scale Space Shuttle.

8. We .... prepared for the simulation by a session in the anti-gravity chair.

9. Your body .... suspended in space and it .... made to move in ways you've never felt before.

10. It's very exciting when you learn that your Space Shuttle .... launched into a simulation orbit.

11. Your space ship .... asked to rendezvous with the International Space Station. There you .... told to perform critical repairs .... carried out.

12. You .... allowed to sit at the control panel and drive the shuttle.

13. The program .... designed by NASA astronauts and is very realistic.

14. When our shuttle .... pulled back into space, I suddenly saw the Earth as the astronauts see it.

17 SCORE

Sport Words

Match the sport to the place where it is played. Be careful: some words you can use twice.

1. court
2. rink
3. table
4. course
5. field
6. ring
7. pitch
8. board
9. track
10. pool

a. American football
b. athletics
c. box
d. chess
e. football
f. golf
g. horse racing
h. ice skating
i. ping-pong
j. swimming
k. tennis
l. cricket
m. baseball
n. squash
o. motor racing

	15

SCORE

Odd Sound Out

▶ Is there an odd vowel sound out or not? If so, circle it.

1. sun	son	blood	tube
2. head	heed	said	bed
3. board	bored	law	floor
4. flood	cup	soup	supper
5. eight	great	head	say
6. glove	truck	dozen	plod
7. found	ground	rowed	house
8. women	sit	village	pretty
9. orange	range	guitar	binge
10. slight	build	busy	rhythm

10 SCORE

Test yourself on kit 12

Right or wrong?

	right	wrong
1. You use the passive only in the past tense.	❑	❑
2. I have be taken on a lovely trip.	❑	❑
3. I am being taken on a lovely trip today.	❑	❑
4. The passive in the conditional tense is: "I would be taken on a lovely trip if I had good friends."	❑	❑
5. The job had been do very quickly.	❑	❑
6. You can always replace the passive by a sentence beginning with "one": One usually drinks beer in a pub.	❑	❑
7. The weather has been turned warm recently.	❑	❑
8. You play golf on a lawn.	❑	❑
9. You play American football on a field.	❑	❑
10. The words **PRETTY** and **SIT** do not have the same vowel sounds.	❑	❑

SCORE: ___ / 10

Answers

Kit 1

page 8
1. am walking 2. say
3. call 4. like
5. graze 6. I'm talking
7. is enjoying 8. loves
9. use 10. are able
11. is tasting 12. makes
13. is jumping 14. invent
15. are coming 16. feels
17. wants

page 10
Action verbs
• dance • dream • have fun
• look at • look for • manage
• run • speak • walk

Verbs to talk about feelings or opinions
• believe • belong • hate
• hear • love • own
• see • think • understand

Present continuous words
• at the moment • now
• tomorrow • tonight

Present simple words
• always • never
• often • sometimes

page 11
1. The, a 2. Ø, a, the
3. A, the, Ø 4. Ø, a, the
5. the, a, an 6. The, the, the, the
7. the, a, the, Ø, the 8. a, a, a
9. An, Ø, the, Ø, the, the
10. an, a, a, Ø, the

page 12
1. packing 2. rushing
3. delay 4. boarding
5. taking off 6. landing
7. picking them up / spending

page 13
1. business 2. minute
3. women 4. build
5. pretty 6. message
7. private 8. village
9. mountains 10. language

page 14
1. right
2. wrong: you use the present simple. **Earthquakes happen...**
3. right
4. wrong: New Zealanders **rear**
5. wrong: **is wearing...**
6. wrong: **is having fun**
7. right
8. wrong: **She speaks English**
9. wrong: **You can spend time and money**
10. right
11. right
12. right

Kit 2

page 16
1. lot 2. some
3. any, a lot of 4. plenty
5. many 6. Most of
7. Most 8. a lot of
9. Most, some, any 10. most
11. any

page 17
1. anywhere 2. nowhere
3. anything 4. something
5. nothing
6. Somebody, anybody
7. nobody 8. somewhere

page 18
1. half, pint 2. landlord
3. tip 4. round
5. lager 6. draught
7. sparkling, fizzy 8. treat
9. dish of the day 10. curry
11. cutlery 12. sweet
13. trifle 14. last orders

page 19
1. sheep 2. meat
3. beer 4. seat
5. team 6. cheap
7. Peak 8. feet
9. people 10. meet
11. greet 12. feel
13. leave

page 20
1. right
2. wrong - There **aren't** many people ...
3. wrong - ... **a few** beers.
4. right
5. wrong - ... **some** books...
6. wrong - ... **any** antiques.
7. wrong - **anywhere** like that...
8. right
9. wrong - It's a type of beer.
10. wrong - They are pronounced the same.

Kit 3

page 22
went, saw, thought, wasn't, broke, found, left, rode, drank, got, bought, ate, began, fought, understood, threw, put.

page 24
1. was born...
2. the teenager James joined
3. He learned...
4. He attacked...
5. This band... committed
6. They justified...
7. Jesse James put together...
8. This new gang began... that frustrated...
9. They robbed... and made off...
10. The gang robbed... and killed many who stood...
11. The James Gang were... and gave money... they met...

Answers

page 25

1. **d**: A. Graham Bell... *telephone*.
2. **h**: The electric light bulb *which was first invented in England in 1800* was finally...
3. **g**: Thomas Alva Edison *whose inventions include* ... lived in New Jersey.
4. **j**: The most famous sewing machine *that we know*... was invented...
5. **c**: The first practical telegraph line *which ran from...*, was invented...
6. **b**: A device *that someone nicknamed the 'Zipper'* was ...
7. **f**: ... very few people knew *what a computer*...
8. **i**: Do you know *which computer*...
9. **a**: The I-POD *which you can use*... is considered by some to be...
10. **e**: Jeff Hawkins invented the palm pilot and did *what we all*...

page 26

- DROP: droplet, dropout, dropper
- PICK: pickup, picky, pickings
- SHAKE: shaker, shake-up, shaky
- LAY: layman, layout, layoff
- HOLD: holder, holding, holdup
- BREAK: breakfast, breakable, daybreak

page 27

t: asked, launched, licked, linked, picked, touched, watched

d: arrived, discovered, finished, imagined, loved, opened

id: distributed, hated, marketed, parted, visited, waited

page 28

1. right
2. wrong: you put the auxiliary in the past and the verb in its basic form: **I didn't go there.**
3. right
4. wrong: you invert the subject and auxiliary and the verb stays in its place: **Did you go there?**
5. wrong: I **was** in the States... and I **thought** it was great.
6. right
7. wrong: **who** invented ...
8. wrong: the car **you bought** or the car **that you bought**
9. wrong: **stop** and **ask** have the **"t"** pronunciation. **Start** and **want** have the **"id"** pronunciation.
10. wrong: it is a **layman**.

Kit 4

page 30

1 b • 2 a • 3 b • 4 b • 5 a • 6 a • 7 b • 8 b

page 31

1. just moved
2. since 1997
3. already seen...
4. never seen
5. for quite
6. yet.
7. Recently
8. I've always

page 32

1. has hosted
2. have been dying
3. have spent
4. decided
5. lined up
6. arranged
7. arrived
8. had
9. started
10. visited
11. she's always been
12. featured
13. have acquired
14. was
15. went
16. had
17. woke up
18. was
19. haven't experienced
20. have decided

page 33

DOWN

1. urgent
2. pain
3. break
4. rescue
5. checkup
6. heal
7. reckless

ACROSS

a. emergency
b. blanket
c. stretcher
d. medicine
e. shout

page 34

1. peek, peak
2. bare, bear
3. plains, planes
4. idle, idol
5. pour, poor
6. heir, air
7. mussels, muscles
8. heard, herd
9. waist, waste
10. allowed, aloud
11. caught, court

page 36

1. wrong
2. wrong: **for** five years
3. right
4. wrong: Why **didn't** you...
5. right
6. wrong: They haven't visited Edinburgh **yet.**
7. right
8. wrong: **for** thousands...
9. wrong: it is what you take to make you better.
10. wrong: you **raise** your voice.
11. right
12. wrong: **Mussels** are seafood.

Kit 5

page 38

1. **I:**... called...
2. **Mrs S:** found, was lying
I: were
3. **Mrs S:** was sleeping, had gone out, was coming, had been
4. **I:** were sleeping, heard
Mrs S: had been murdered.
5. **I:** did you do
Mrs S: picked
6. **I:** had been killed
7. **Mrs S:** didn't do

page 40

1. **d**: Before ... I had been living...
2. **h**: I had decided... before I actually...
3. **l**: I was afraid... and was constantly...
4. **a** I needed to be ...because things...
5. **g**: I had asked... but the ones...

Answers

6. **b** : The loneliness... when I met...
7. **i**: She had just ...and she wanted...`
8. **c**: I was... when I saw her...
9. **k**: She was taking... and seemed...
10. **f**: We had already... but this time...
11. **e**: Last night...even though ...

page 41

1. Jane: do, made 2. John: do
3. Jane: do 4. John: do
5. Jane: made 6. John: do
7. Jane: do 8. John: make
9. Jane: make 10. John: do, make
11. Jane: make 12. John: done, make

page 42

1. Sophisticated 2. Expensive
3. Rushed 4. Casual
5. Stressful 6. Policemen
7. Downtown 8. Convenient
9. Fashionable 10. Traffic
11. Luxury 12. Trendy

page 43

1. d - divorced 2. i - important
3. b - extraordinary 4. g - warning
5. h - recording 6. e - forceful
7. f - endorsement 8. c - boredom
9. a - coarseness

page 44

1. wrong: **was sleeping/heard**
2. right
3. wrong: **They worked**...
4. wrong: She **was having** a bath
5. wrong: when I **called** you?
6. right
7. wrong: Have you **made**
8. wrong: What did you **do**
9. wrong: It is easy and occurs at the right time for you.
10. wrong: casual clothing is very relaxed.
11. wrong: FANCY means very elaborate.
12. right

Kit 6

page 46

1. He is going to take a cab.
2. They are going to go up in the wheel.
3. They are going to watch a match.
4. She is going to buy a travelcard.
5. They are going to see a show.
6. He is going to steal the bag.
7. Will you...
8. Shall I...
9. Will you...

page 47

1. **How** will they cope... ?
2. **Who** will increase funding... ?
3. **How many** more people are going to live in London...?
4. **What else** will be created...?
5. **What** are we going to buy?
6. **Why** are we going to buy... ?
7. **When** are you going to visit...?
8. **How long** is it going to take to get from London to Paris...?
9. **Where** will you be coming from?
10. **How old** is the Tower of London?

page 48

1. skyscraper 2. suburbs
3. storey 4. passers-by
5. pavement 6. gutter
7. pillar box 8. cashpoint
9. gridlock 10. mugging

page 49

1.d 2.a 3.i
4.e 5.b 6.j
7.g 8.c 9.h
10.f

page 50

1. wrong: **going to**
2. wrong: **shall**
3. wrong: **Will you/Are you going to come** tonight?
4. wrong: **will**
5. right
6. wrong: When **do you think**
7. wrong: **Where** are you coming **from**?
8. wrong: How long have you been waiting here?
9. right
10. wrong: it is a floor in a building. The synonym of TALE is STORY.
11. wrong: **going to**
12. right

Kit 7

page 52

1. you obey 2. I had known
3. I would take 4. I'll try and find
5. would you say? 6. don't mind
7. would have been 8. hadn't shaped
9. see 10. have

page 53

1. a 2. c 3. a
4. b 5. c 6. b
7. a 8. c 9. a
10. b

page 54

- check-up, checkout, checkmate
- soundproof, soundtrack, unsound, soundless
- end-result, dead-end, endless, ending
- freeloader, freehand, freelance, freeway

page 55

1. famous 2. display
3. raise 4. decade
5. shaker 6. major
7. amazing 8. stage
9. today 10. frame
11. painting 12. nation

page 56

1. wrong: WILL is used to express a possibility.
2. wrong: **If I had lived in New York, I would have been happy.**

Answers

3. right
4. wrong: If it **rains, I'll** take...
5. right
6. wrong: ... **as fascinating as...**
7. right
8. wrong: ... **worse than....**
9. wrong: the correct word is **mindless.**
10. wrong: they do have the same vowel sound, the same as in "late".

Kit 8

page 58

1. **can** I get
2. **can** visit
3. will **be able to**
4. What **can**
5. **must** take
6. It **must** be
7. **could** go..., **might** prefer..., **must** be..., **don't have to...** You **could** do...
8. **couldn't** possibly ... **can't** do ...
9. **can't** ... **don't have to** ... **can**
10. **Can** you... **might** check it ...
11. You **can**..., I **might**...

page 59

1.**After** 75 million years...
2.... **until** 1884.
3.... **at** 9 a.m. **in** summer.
4.**On** June 26th ...
5.**During** prehistoric times...
6....opened **since** 1987.
7.... **for** four years ...
8.**Before** 1987...
9....**from** 9 a.m. to 9 p.m.....
10.**Within** 10 million years ...

page 60

1. freezing -> **g**
2. drizzly -> **j**
3. cloudy -> **c**
4. windy -> **a**
5. stormy -> **f**
6. showers -> **i**
7. black ice -> **e**
8. pouring -> **d**
9. lightning -> **b**
10. thunder -> **h**

page 61

Toronto • ● •
beaver ● •
maple leaf ● ••
Mounted Police ● • • ●
Eskimos ● ••
Aboriginals ••● ••
Inuits ● •
Freezing ● •
Two million lakes ●●•●
Grizzly bears ● •●

page 62

1. wrong: Canadians **can speak**
2. right
3. wrong: **will be able to**
4. wrong: it is less sure
5. wrong: it means you are not being forced to go
6. wrong: they mean the same thing
7. wrong: **on Monday**
8. wrong: **First**
9. wrong: it's raining just a little
10. wrong: the **second** syllable is stressed

Kit 9

page 64

1. from attending
2. of contravening
3. to go
4. to house
5. to living
6. from seeing
7. to release
8. living
9. to have
10. to change
11. to accept
12. for helping
13. to open
14. to open

page 65

1. on
2. in front of
3. in
4. near
5. behind
6. under
7. over
8. around
9. among
10. towards
11. across

page 66

1. traffic light
2. hangover
3. call me on the phone
4. pickup truck
5. shortly
6. trunk
7. hood
8. long difficult walk
9. sold
10. thingamajig

page 68

1. town
2. down
3. crowded
4. mountain
5. found
6. sound
7. proud
8. drought
9. frown
10. house
11. loud
12. round

page 68

1. wrong: It's worth **going** on a safari...
2. wrong: **I wanted him to take** me ...
3. right
4. right
5. wrong: I'm looking forward **to hearing**
6. right
7. right
8. wrong: he is close to them.
9. wrong: you get a hangover when you drink too much.
10. right

Kit 10

page 70

1. Many people frequently come...
2. They build the city very quickly,...
3. They usually use...
4. Each person creates his contribution very carefully...
5. Money is not allowed so people give each other food freely.
6. The atmosphere is very friendly and you can speak to people easily.
7. Many people come with strange and funny cars that they build specially to show...
8. These vehicles are sometimes
9. The Nevada desert is clearly ...
10. Tourists generally don't know....
11. At the end of the week, they

Answers

always...

12. On the last day, you can see everything slowly turning...

page 71

1. directly 2. in a very friendly way
3. too fast 4. easy
5. easily 6. hard
7. hardly 8. Her playing was lovely
9. slowly and surely
10. really

page 72

1. hammer 2. screw
3. screwdriver 4. saw
5. drill 6. brush
7. plane 8. clamp
9. scissors

page 73

wind (as in sit) • air that blows very hard

wind (as in five) • to turn a rope around sthg

tear (as in air) • to rip

tear (as in beer) • what you have in your eye...

deSERT • to abandon

DEsert • a place like the Sahara

lead (as in feed) : • to be at the head of a group

lead (as in bed) • a heavy metal

polish (as in so) • people from Poland

polish (as in pop) • to rub and make shine

PRESent • a gift

preSENT • to give some information...

bow (as in so) • what you use with arrows

bow (as in cow) : • to bend very low

CONcert • a musical evening

conCERT • to work with other people to get their agreement

Close (s like a z) • to shut down something

Close (s like ss) • very near

row (as in so) • to make a boat go forward with oars

row (as in cow) • an argument

page 74

1. wrong: the adverbs go **after** the verb "to be".
2. wrong: adverbs of **frequency** go **before** the verb, **adverbs of manner after**.
3. right
4. wrong: I **never make** mistakes...
5. wrong: he understood everything very **fast**.
6. right
7. wrong: I **hardly know** him.
8. wrong: you use a screwdriver with screws and a hammer with nails.
9. wrong: you use a saw
10. wrong: the verb "to **lead**" has the same vowel sound as **tea**, and the heavy metal **"lead"** has the same sound as **bed**.

Kit 11

page 76

1. The journalist replied that **he would of course be surprised.** He wondered how fast this change **had been.**
2. The economist answered that ten years ago Ireland **had been reputed...** He continued by saying that today the Irish economy **was booming.**
3. The journalist wanted to know **what had happened.**
4. The economist said that in a few words the situation **could be explained** by ...
5. The journalist went on to ask how the economy **was doing** at the moment.
6. The economist replied that the Irish economy **was** the...
7. The journalist said **he thought** transport **was** very bad.
8. The economist replied that thanks to...superhighways distance... **had been abolished.**
9. The journalist asked the economist **to tell him** about Dublin.
10. He said that Dublin **had become** one of the ...
11. The journalist wondered if everything **had gone** easily,...
12. The economist explained that naturally all this **had not come** without problems; the vast influx of capital...**had put** ...
13. The journalist wanted to know if the Irish **were regretting** this ...
14. The economist told her **he had** to be kidding. He added that after centuries of being on the fringe of Europe, Ireland was now at the centre. He said that the Celtic Tiger looked set to keep roaring.

page 78

1. He said to his fellow worke: "Look at the dolphin!"
2." He is escorting the town's fishing boats to and from port."
3. Kevin Flannery said: "I'm going to officially record the dolphin...."
4. Paddy told the tourists: "The dolphin has developed into a playful..."
5. A child asked: "What is the dolphin's name?"
6. Paddy said: "It's Fungie."
7. One tourist asked Paddy: "Is Fungie a social outcast?"
8. Paddy replied: "No, he's not. He often meets other dolphins..."
9. "Thousands of visitors have been coming to Dingle Bay ever since Fungie arrived. I hope it will continue."

page 79

1. tell 2. tell 3. Tell
4. say 5. say 6. telling
7. told 8. say, says, tell
9. say, tell, said 10. tell

Answers

page 80

1. b
2. d
3. i
4. k
5. l
6. f
7. m
8. a
9. e
10. c
11. g
12. j
13. h

page 81

1. says
2. seldom
3. never
4. lie
5. light
6. silent
7. house
8. how
9. mouth.
10. break
11. day.
12. Praise

page 82

1. wrong: He asked what Ireland **was** like ...
2. wrong: You don't always have to put it into the past perfect.
3. wrong: He asked **if** the Irish economy...
4. right
5. wrong: He advised people **to go** to Ireland.
6. wrong:... to **tell** the time.
7. wrong: **telling** jokes.
8. wrong: He **told me** he was happy/He **said** he was happy.
9. wrong: You improve the way it works with new hardware and software.
10. right

Kit 12

Page 84

1. are being taken
2. is known
3. have been made
4. is offered
5. can be seen
6. have been built
7. Is located
8. have been included
9. are constantly being damaged
10. are being served
11. has been organized

Page 85

1. are welcomed
2. was given
3. be made
4. are taken
5. will be briefed
6. have been fitted out
7. I was put
8. had been prepared
9. is suspended/is made
10. is going to be launched
11. is asked /are told /are going to be carried out
12. are allowed
13. was designed
14. was being pulled back

Page 86

1. k.& n. tennis, squash court
2. h. ice skating rink
3. i. ping-pong table
4. f. golf course
5. a.& m. American football, baseball field
6. c. box
7. e. & l. football, cricket pitch
8. d. chess board
9. b. , o & g. athletics, motor racing and horse racing track
10. j. swimming pool

Page 87

1. tube
2. heed
3. no odd sound out
4. soup
5. head
6. plod
7. rowed
8. no odd sound out
9. range
10. slight

Page 88

1. wrong: you can use the passive in all tenses.
2. wrong: I have **been** taken ...
3. correct.
4. correct.
5. wrong: the job had been **done**...
6. wrong: we don't usually use "one" in making sentences in English. It's better to use the passive.
7. wrong: the weather **has turned** warm...
8. wrong: you play golf on a **course**.
9. right.
10. wrong: they do have the same vowel sound.

Coordination éditoriale : Lucie Grimal
Conception graphique : Judith de Beco

Achevé d'imprimer en Espagne par Graficas Estella
Dépôt légal éditeur : 62120-09/2005
Édition 1
Librairie Générale Française - 31, rue de Fleurus - 75278 Paris Cedex 6
ISBN : 2-253-01639-X

30/1639/1